Christmas Is Coming!

AN ADVENT BOOK

Text copyright © 2019 by Chronicle Books LLC.

Illustrations copyright © 2019 by Katie Hickey.

Raspberry Hot Chocolate recipe on page 3 © 2019 by Shelly Westerhausen.

Material on page 12 previously published in *Very Merry Cookie Party* by Barbara Grunes and Virginia Van Vynckt (text copyright © 2010 by Barbara Grunes and Virginia Van Vynckt) by Chronicle Books LLC.

Material on pages 32-33 previously published in *Vegetarian Heartland* by Shelly Westerhausen (text copyright © 2017 by Shelly Westerhausen) by Chronicle Books LLC.

The Elves and the Shoemaker is based on the story by The Brothers Grimm.

The Nutcracker is based on the story by E. T. A. Hoffman.

Library of Congress Cataloging-in-Publication Data available.

ISBN 978-1-4521-7407-5

Manufactured in China.

Design by Amelia Mack.

Typeset in Recoleta, Plantin, and Brandon Grotesque.

The illustrations in this book were rendered in watercolor.

10 9 8 7 6 5 4

Chronicle books and gifts are available at special quantity discounts to corporations, professional associations, literacy programs, and other organizations. For details and discount information, please contact our premiums department at corporatesales@chroniclebooks.com or at 1-800-759-0190.

Chronicle Books LLC
680 Second Street
San Francisco, California 94107

Chronicle Books—we see things differently.
Become part of our community at www.chroniclekids.com.

Christmas Is Coming!

AN ADVENT BOOK

ILLUSTRATED BY KATIE HICKEY

chronicle books · san francisco

TABLE OF CONTENTS

Letter to Santa

Santa Claus loves to receive letters every year from kids like you.
Is there a special gift you've been hoping for? Or would you like
to tell Santa all about your wishes and dreams for the year ahead?
Maybe you want to add some drawings, too! If you need a little help
with the writing, ask a parent or an older sibling to write down what
you would like to say to Santa. When you've finished your note, sign
your name and ask your parent to help you mail the letter. Don't
forget to address the envelope!

Deck the Halls

Deck the halls with boughs of holly, Fa la la la la la la la la!
'Tis the season to be jolly, Fa la la la la la la la la!
Don we now our gay apparel, Fa la la la la la la la la!
Troll the ancient Yuletide carol, Fa la la la la la la la la!

See the blazing yule before us, Fa la la la la la la la la!
Strike the harp and join the chorus, Fa la la la la la la la la!
Follow me in merry measure, Fa la la la la la la la la!
While I tell of Yuletide treasure, Fa la la la la la la la la!

Fast away the old year passes, Fa la la la la la la la la!
Hail the new, ye lads and lasses, Fa la la la la la la la la!
Sing we joyous all together! Fa la la la la la la la la!
Heedless of the wind and weather, Fa la la la la la la la la!

Raspberry Hot Chocolate

This rich hot chocolate comes together in just a few minutes and gets its sweetness from the addition of raspberry jam.

2 cups (480 millilitres) whole milk
¼ cup (80 grams) unsweetened cocoa powder
¼ cup (75 grams) raspberry jam
   (preferably seedless)
½ tsp vanilla extract
Whipped cream for topping (optional)

In a medium saucepan, combine the milk and cocoa powder. Whisk constantly over medium-low heat until the cocoa powder is completely dissolved and bubbles start to form around the edge of the milk mixture, about 3 to 5 minutes. Turn off the heat and whisk in the raspberry jam and vanilla extract.

Pour evenly between two mugs, top with whipped cream (if using), and serve.

Makes 2 servings

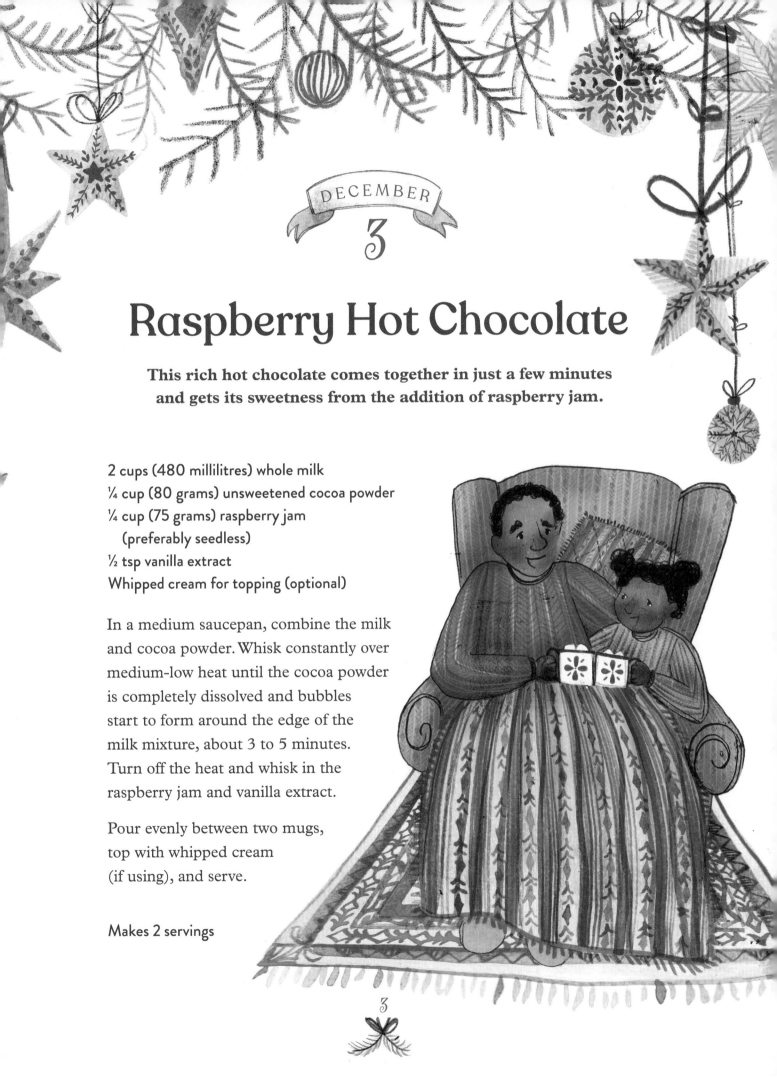

Paper Snowflakes

Materials

White paper (option to use shiny or
    patterned craft or origami paper)

Scissors

Toothpick or hole punch

String

Begin with a square piece of paper. Fold the paper in half
diagonally to make a triangle. Fold the triangle in half.
Fold the triangle into thirds, making sure that the sides
line up. This can be tricky, so don't crease the paper until
the folds are just right.

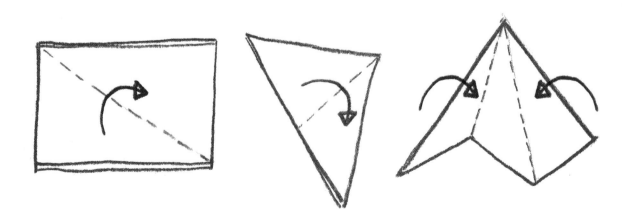

Trim the points off the bottom of the triangle. Cut into
the folds from either side. Experiment by making your
cuts a variety of shapes and sizes. Be sure not to cut
all the way across the triangle. Gently unfold to reveal
your snowflake!

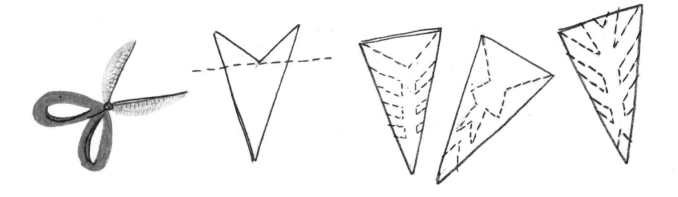

Use a toothpick or hole punch to make a hole on one
point of the snowflake. Thread string through the hole to
make a hanging loop. Use your snowflakes to decorate
windows, walls, or the branches of your Christmas tree!

Find in this scene:

6 geese   The girl mailing a letter
3 hens   The couple getting engaged
3 snowmen   The dog stealing a pie
10 sleds   The cat on the roof

Mystery Carol

Materials
Large pad of paper
Markers (use washable markers if you have younger players)

Gather family and friends for a guess-the-carol drawing game! To play, one person thinks of a Christmas carol and then tries to draw the carol's name while the other players try to guess which one it is. If the title is too hard or you don't know it, try drawing the lyrics from the song instead. Younger players may need a whispered suggestion—something simple like "We Three Kings" or "Frosty the Snowman." Let older players tackle trickier carols like "Silent Night."

A larger group can divide into two teams. Both play at the same time. Each team selects a team member to draw first. Whichever team guesses its carol first is the winner for that round. This can get noisy!

Suggested carols

Angels We Have Heard on High

Carol of the Bells

Deck the Halls

Go Tell It on the Mountain

God Rest Ye Merry Gentlemen

Good King Wenceslas

I Saw Three Ships

Jingle Bells

O Christmas Tree

Rudolph the Red-Nosed Reindeer

Santa Claus Is Coming to Town

The Little Drummer Boy

The Twelve Days of Christmas

Up on the Housetop

White Christmas

Spare Stocking

Materials

Felt	Tape
Scissors	White glue
Small hole punch	Paper
Red yarn	Markers

Brush off your craft skills to make an extra stocking for a pet or Christmas visitor. Or fill your handmade stocking with a few small gifts and give to a special friend or teacher!

1. Put together two pieces of felt and cut out a stocking shape. Hold the two pieces together and punch holes about ½ inch (12 millimetres) apart along all the edges except the top.

2. Measure all the way around the edge with red yarn, and cut the yarn to four times that length. Make a knot in one end. Wrap the other end tightly with a piece of tape so it looks like a shoelace.

3. Starting at the top front hole, lace up the stocking. Leave a loop of yarn for hanging.

4. Decorate the stocking by gluing on paper or felt cutouts. Make a paper nameplate to glue to the top.

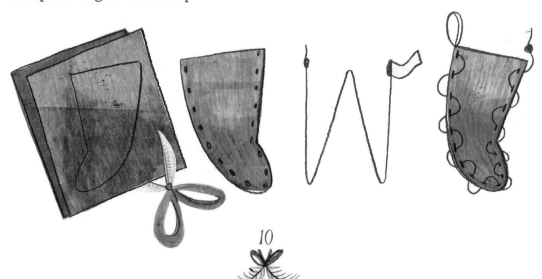

10

Snowball Cookies

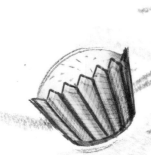

1 cup (220 grams) unsalted butter, at room temperature
½ cup (60 grams) confectioners' sugar, plus 1 cup (120 grams)
   sifted for rolling
¼ teaspoon ground cinnamon
¼ teaspoon salt
2¼ cups (310 grams) all-purpose flour
1 cup (120 grams) ground walnuts

1. Preheat the oven to 350°Fahrenheit (180°Celsius). Have ready two ungreased cookie sheets.

2. In a large bowl, with an electric mixer on medium speed, beat together the butter, ½ cup (60 grams) confectioners' sugar, the cinnamon, and salt until smooth and creamy, about 2 minutes. On low speed, gradually beat in the flour and then the nuts just until mixed. The dough will be stiff and somewhat crumbly.

3. Pinch off pieces of the dough and roll between your palms into 1-inch (2.5-centimetre) balls. Place on the cookie sheets, spacing them about 1½ inches (4 centimetre) apart.

4. Bake in the center of the oven until the tops are set to the touch and the bottoms are lightly golden, about 10 minutes. Let the cookies cool on the cookie sheets until they are still warm but are firm enough to handle without crumbling.

5. Spread 1 cup (120 grams) sifted confectioners' sugar on a plate. Roll the warm cookies in the sugar, coating them evenly. Set on wire racks to cool completely. When the cookies have cooled, roll them again lightly in the sugar.

6. Store in an airtight container at room temperature for up to 1 week.

Makes about 50 cookies

Spread Christmas Cheer

Play Santa this Christmas—put together a care package for a child or family in need of some extra Christmas cheer.

With the help of your parents, church, or school, locate a family in need. You could also do some research online to choose a charity or organization that can help connect you with a child who otherwise will not be receiving presents this year. Local hospitals or shelters are a great place to start.

Find out the age of the child, and then start assembling your care package. Younger children might enjoy gently used books or toys you've outgrown. Or, with your saved allowance, maybe you can buy a new toy or two. Add a couple treats, like a candy cane or chocolate kisses. Finish up with a handmade Christmas card.

Put all the items in a box and wrap it like a present. Bring the box to the agency or location that will deliver it. Now that's the spirit of Christmas!

Jingle Bells

Dashing through the snow
In a one-horse open sleigh,
O'er the fields we go,
Laughing all the way.
Bells on bobtails ring,
Making spirits bright,
What fun it is to ride and sing
A sleighing song tonight!

Jingle bells, jingle bells,
Jingle all the way.
Oh what fun it is to ride
In a one-horse open sleigh, hey!
Jingle bells, jingle bells,
Jingle all the way.
Oh what fun it is to ride
In a one-horse open sleigh!

Now the ground is white,
Go it while you're young.
Take the girls tonight
And sing this sleighing song.
Just get a bobtailed bay,
Two forty as his speed,
Hitch him to an open sleigh
And crack, you'll take the lead!

Jingle bells, jingle bells,
Jingle all the way.
Oh what fun it is to ride
In a one-horse open sleigh, hey!
Jingle bells, jingle bells,
Jingle all the way.
Oh what fun it is to ride
In a one-horse open sleigh!

Wise Advisors

In honor of the Three Wise Men, imagine that you could choose three people to call on for advice whenever you liked. Your "wise men" could be any gender, of any age, and from any period in history. They could be famous, or they could be people you know. Who would you pick? What advice would you ask for? Write the three names you come up with on a piece of paper.

Ask your family members to do the same and then go around the table and have each person introduce their wise advisors and explain why they picked these three people.

18

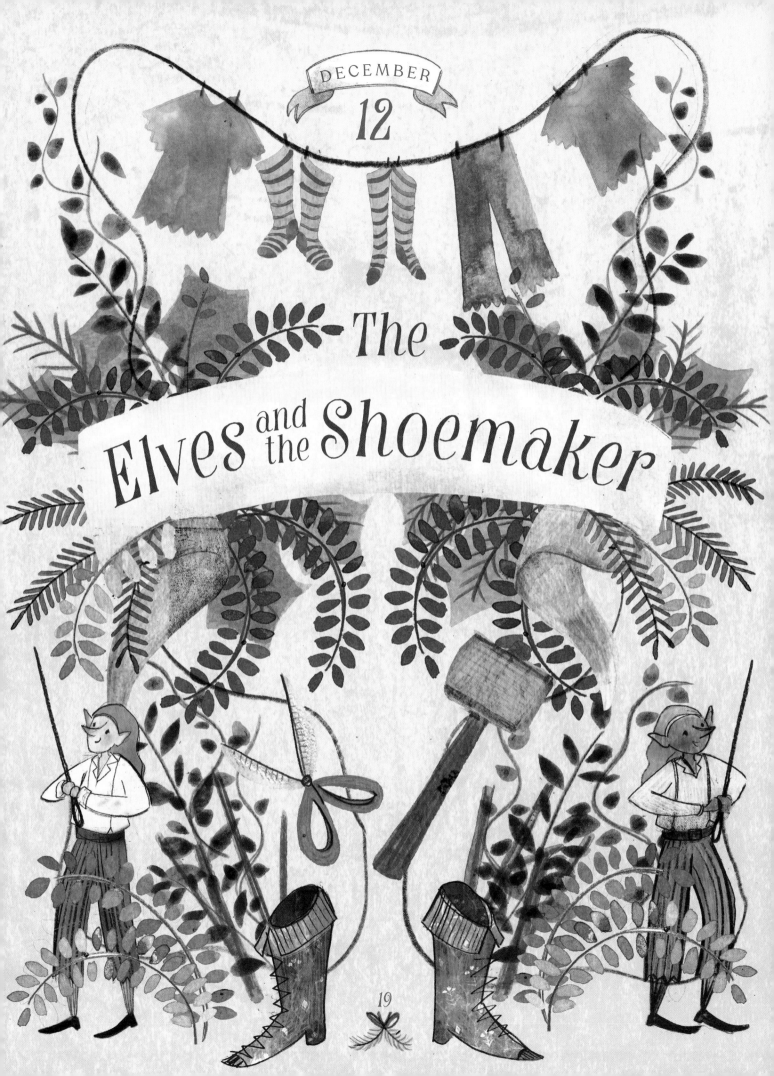

DECEMBER

12

The
Elves and the Shoemaker

19

THERE ONCE was a kind old shoemaker and his wife who had fallen on hard times and had become very poor. Finally, on a cold winter's morning, the shoemaker found he had only enough leather for one pair of shoes. "I must take great care in their making," said the shoemaker to his wife. "For if they do not sell, there will be nothing to eat."

The shoemaker spent the afternoon tracing a design and cutting the leather, but his heart was heavy and his fingers moved slowly. When evening came, he laid the pieces of leather out on his worktable. He would finish making up the shoes in the morning, after a good night's sleep. But he slept poorly and had strange dreams where silver thread, bright ribbons, and polished leather danced before his eyes.

When morning came, his wife woke early to put on the kettle. Passing the worktable, she gave a cry that woke the shoemaker straight away. Rushing down the stairs, he followed his wife's gaze to the table, upon which sat the most astonishing shoes either of them had ever seen! They were sewn with silver thread, laced with ribbons, and polished so they gleamed. They were beautiful—but where had they come from? Having nothing else to sell, and no money for more leather, the couple put the shoes in the window of the shop, and waited, as they always did, for customers that never came.

But not five minutes had passed before a man strode into the shop. He was dressed from head to toe in brightly colored fabrics with more buckles and buttons than the cobbler could count. "The shoes in your window are magnificent," he said. "I must have them, at once!" The shoes fit him so well that he insisted on paying double the price. The shoemaker couldn't believe his luck—this was enough to pay for the leather for two more pairs of shoes! But after all the excitement, he only had time to cut out the leather and lay the pieces on the table before it was time for bed. This night was just as strange as the last, and his dreams were full of odd shapes and patterns.

In the morning, the shoemaker and his wife crept downstairs together and could scarcely believe their eyes: The pieces of leather had once again been transformed! On the worktable sat two pairs of the oddest shoes they had ever seen. They were cut in a most unusual style, and had intriguing patterns sewn all over the leather. Again, the shoemaker had nothing else to sell, so he put the shoes in the shop window. An elegant woman and her daughter saw the shoes and swept into the shop to purchase them to wear to a party that evening. "These must be the latest new style," said the woman, as she and her daughter paid double for the shoes.

The shoemaker now had enough to buy leather for four new pairs of shoes. It took him all afternoon to cut the leather, and with hope in his heart, he left the shoes on the worktable and went to bed. Sure enough, in the morning, four smart-looking pairs of shoes awaited him on his worktable, and all four sold for more than they were worth. That night, the shoemaker's wife bought enough food to cook a modest feast, and the couple ate heartily for the first time in many days.

And so it went, day after day, until the shoemaker and his wife were prosperous once more. As their fortunes improved, the couple grew curious about how these shoes came to be. So one evening, they left out a few pieces of leather and hid themselves very well behind some coats hanging beside the worktable.

At the darkest hour of the night, they heard a scuffling sound and peeked between the coats to see two little figures skipping across the room. Their feet were bare and their clothes were patched and worn, but their faces were merry as they hoisted themselves up to the table and set about measuring and stitching and gluing the pieces of leather, until many fine pairs of shoes were neatly laid out. Then the elves, for that is what they were, jumped from the table and, giggling, snuck away out the window.

The next day, the shoemaker's wife said, "Why don't we do something kind for these elves who have helped us so much? They haven't got any shoes of their own or any nice clothes to wear." So the shoemaker made two small pairs of boots, and his wife sewed two pairs of pants, and two warm little jackets and caps. They laid out the clothes and shoes and took their hiding places behind the coats.

Just as before, the elves slipped in through the window and climbed upon the worktable. When they saw the gifts, they stood still with shock, but then each let out a whoop of glee. Eagerly, they set about putting on the clothes and boots, singing, "Now we are so fine to see, no longer cobblers shall we be!" They leapt and danced happily around the room, before stealing away into the night.

The elves were never seen again. But from that day on, the shoemaker and his wife lived comfortably and happily together for the rest of their days.

THE END

Christmas Jokes

Q: Where do snowmen keep their money?

A: In a snow bank.

Q: Who has a jolly laugh, brings you presents, and scratches up your furniture?

A: Santa Claws.

Q: How does a sheep say "Merry Christmas"?

A: "Fleece Navidad!"

Q: What did one snowman say to the other snowman?

A: Do you smell carrots?

Q: What did the hat say to the scarf?

A: You hang around while I go on a head.

Q: Why are Christmas trees such bad knitters?

A: They are always dropping their needles.

Q: Which of Santa's reindeer has bad manners?

A: Rude-olph!

Q: What is a librarian's favorite Christmas song?

A: "Silent Night"

Q: How is the Christmas alphabet different from the ordinary alphabet?

A: The Christmas alphabet has NO EL.

The Twelve Days of Christmas

On the first day of Christmas,
My true love gave to me
A partridge in a pear tree.

On the second day of Christmas,
My true love gave to me
Two turtle doves,
And a partridge in a pear tree.

On the third day of Christmas,
My true love gave to me
Three French hens,
Two turtle doves,
And a partridge in a pear tree.

On the fourth day of Christmas,
My true love gave to me
Four calling birds,
Three French hens,
Two turtle doves,
And a partridge in a pear tree.

On the fifth day of Christmas,
My true love gave to me
Five golden rings,
Four calling birds,
Three French hens,
Two turtle doves,
And a partridge in a pear tree.

On the sixth day of Christmas,
My true love gave to me
Six geese a-laying,
Five golden rings,
Four calling birds,
Three French hens,
Two turtle doves,
And a partridge in a pear tree.

On the seventh day of Christmas,
My true love gave to me
Seven swans a-swimming,
Six geese a-laying,
Five golden rings,
Four calling birds,
Three French hens,
Two turtle doves,
And a partridge in a pear tree.

On the eighth day of Christmas,
My true love gave to me
Eight maids a-milking,
Seven swans a-swimming,
Six geese a-laying,
Five golden rings,
Four calling birds,
Three French hens,
Two turtle doves,
And a partridge in a pear tree.

On the ninth day of Christmas,
My true love gave to me
Nine ladies dancing,
Eight maids a-milking,
Seven swans a-swimming,
Six geese a-laying,
Five golden rings,
Four calling birds,
Three French hens,
Two turtle doves,
And a partridge in a pear tree.

On the tenth day of Christmas,
My true love gave to me
Ten lords a-leaping,
Nine ladies dancing,
Eight maids a-milking,
Seven swans a-swimming,
Six geese a-laying,
Five golden rings,
Four calling birds,
Three French hens,
Two turtle doves,
And a partridge in a pear tree.

On the eleventh day of Christmas,
My true love gave to me
Eleven pipers piping,
Ten lords a-leaping,
Nine ladies dancing,
Eight maids a-milking,
Seven swans a-swimming,
Six geese a-laying,
Five golden rings,
Four calling birds,
Three French hens,
Two turtle doves,
And a partridge in a pear tree.

On the twelfth day of Christmas,
My true love gave to me
Twelve drummers drumming,
Eleven pipers piping,
Ten lords a-leaping,
Nine ladies dancing,
Eight maids a-milking,
Seven swans a-swimming,
Six geese a-laying,
Five golden rings,
Four calling birds,
Three French hens,
Two turtle doves,
And a partridge in a pear tree!

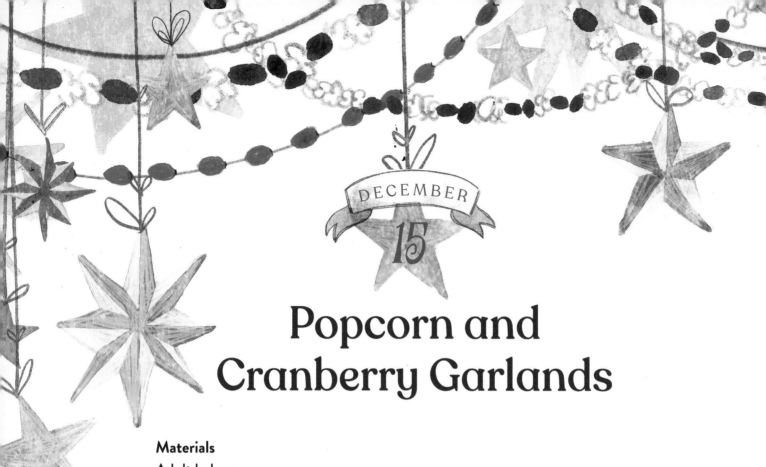

Popcorn and Cranberry Garlands

Materials
Adult helper
Sturdy, large-eyed needle
Heavy thread or unscented dental floss
Scissors
Dried cranberries
Freshly popped popcorn without butter or salt

1. Ask an adult helper to select a needle with a large eye.

2. Cut a piece of thread 7 feet (2 metres) long and thread it onto the needle. Double it over and make a thick knot at the end. Make a second knot about 4 inches (10 centimetres) from the end.

3. Carefully push the needle through a cranberry or popcorn kernel, making sure to insert the needle through a thicker part of the kernel. Alternate groups of popcorn and cranberries, stringing them onto your thread until there's only 4 inches (10 centimetres) of thread left.

4. Tie the strand off with a big, tight knot. Your garland is ready to drape on the tree!

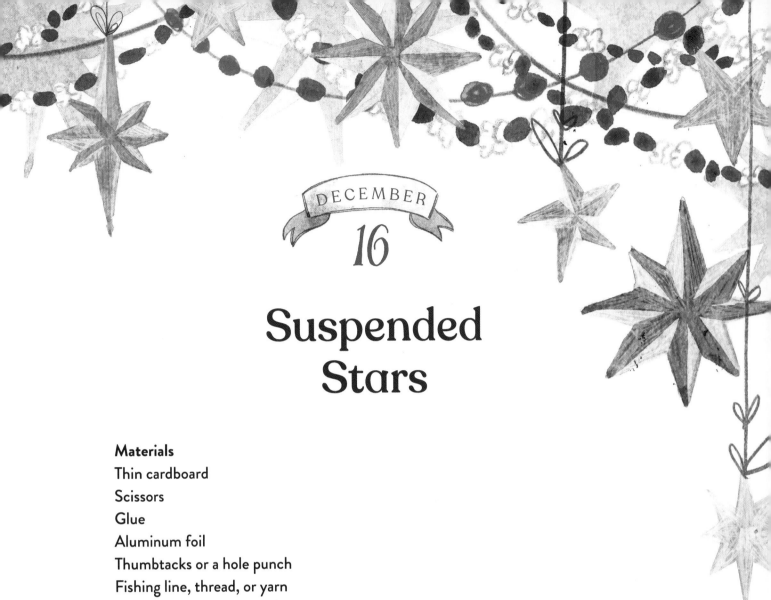

16

Suspended Stars

Materials
Thin cardboard
Scissors
Glue
Aluminum foil
Thumbtacks or a hole punch
Fishing line, thread, or yarn

1. Cut out stars of various sizes from thin cardboard.

2. Apply glue to one side of a cardboard star, and place it glue-side down on a sheet of aluminum foil. Carefully cut the foil around the edge of the star and fold any excess aluminum around the star to create neat edges. Turn over the star and repeat this process so that both sides of the star are covered in foil.

3. Poke a hole at the top of the star with a thumbtack. Push a piece of fishing line through the hole and knot the ends. Alternatively, you can make your hole with a hole punch and use thread or yarn in place of fishing line.

4. Suspend your stars from the ceiling or around a window using thumbtacks.

Chocolate Gingerbread Bars

**These brownie-like bars are inspired by classic gingerbread
cut-out cookies and are delicious plain or frosted.**

1 cup (220 grams) unsalted butter
½ cup (160 grams) molasses
1 cup (200 grams) packed light brown sugar
½ teaspoon vanilla extract
3 eggs
1½ teaspoon ground ginger
1 Tablespoon ground cinnamon
½ teaspoon fine sea salt
½ teaspoon ground cloves
¼ cup (20 grams) Dutch-process cocoa powder
1¾ cups (245 grams) all-purpose flour
½ cup (90 grams) semisweet chocolate chips

Frosting
2 ounces (55 grams) cream cheese,
    at room temperature
4 Tablespoons (55 grams) unsalted butter,
    at room temperature
3½ Tablespoons eggnog
¾ cup (90 grams) powdered sugar

Ground cinnamon for dusting

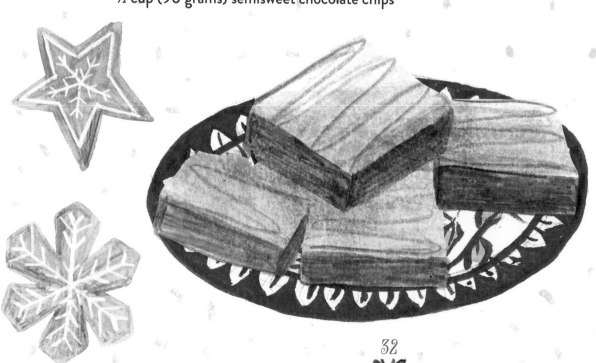

Preheat the oven to 350°Fahrenheit (180°Celsius). Line a 9-by-13-inch (23-by-33-centimetre) baking pan with parchment paper.

In a medium saucepan over medium heat, melt the butter. Remove from the heat and whisk in the molasses, brown sugar, and vanilla. Let cool for 5 minutes and then whisk in the eggs.

In a small bowl, whisk together the ginger, cinnamon, salt, cloves, cocoa powder, and flour. Make a well in the center of the dry ingredients and pour the molasses mixture into the center. Gradually stir the molasses mixture into the dry ingredients until combined. Fold in the chocolate chips. Pour the batter into the prepared baking pan.

Bake until the center is set, about 25 minutes. Let cool completely.

To make the frosting: Meanwhile, in the bowl of a stand mixer fitted with the whisk attachment, beat the cream cheese and butter on medium speed until completely smooth, about 1 minute. With the mixer running, slowly pour in the eggnog and beat just until combined. Turn the speed to low, slowly pour in the powdered sugar, and beat until a thick frosting forms, about 3 minutes.

Spread the glaze over the gingerbread with a spatula or offset knife and dust with cinnamon. Let stand until the glaze begins to harden, about 10 minutes. Cut into squares and serve.

Hide and Sing

This irresistibly fun singing game for the whole family is a festive version of the game hot-and-cold!

First, get the family together to choose a few Christmas carols that everyone knows.

Let each family member take a turn being "It." It leaves the room for a few minutes. The other family members choose a hiding spot for a candy cane, home-baked goodie, or a tiny gift. Then It is called back into the room.

As It enters the room, the other family members softly sing a Christmas carol. As It gets closer to the treat, the family sings more loudly. If It moves further from the treat, everyone sings more softly. Of course, It gets to keep the treat once he or she finds it.

Silent Night

Silent night, holy night,
All is calm, all is bright
Round yon virgin mother and child.
Holy infant, so tender and mild,
Sleep in heavenly peace,
Sleep in heavenly peace.

Silent night, holy night,
Shepherds quake at the sight;
Glories stream from heaven afar,
Heavenly hosts sing Alleluia!
Christ the Savior is born,
Christ the Savior is born!

Silent night, holy night,
Son of God, love's pure light;
Radiant beams from thy holy face
With the dawn of redeeming grace,
Jesus, Lord, at thy birth,
Jesus, Lord, at thy birth.

ON CHRISTMAS EVE, a little girl named Marie peeked out the window of her nursery to watch the snow falling outside. It was the night of her family's Christmas party, Marie's favorite night of all the year. Tonight, friends and family would arrive dressed in their finest, and the house would be filled with music, laughter, and dancing.

Marie and her younger brother Fritz had been asked to wait in the nursery until all was ready. Just when they couldn't bear to wait any longer, the doors of the nursery were flung open. In the doorway was a tall figure, wrapped in a magnificent cloak. "Godfather Drosselmeyer!" the children called, running to him. Their godfather was a mysterious man, but always brought the children the most wonderful presents and stories from his travels in faraway lands.

This year, Godfather Drosselmeyer gave Fritz a set of fine toy soldiers. And for Marie, he produced from under his cloak a strange doll, dressed like a soldier in a smart red jacket, with big eyes and a wide grin. It was a nutcracker, Drosselmeyer explained, showing Marie how the little man's strong jaws could crack any nut. Marie loved the Nutcracker at once.

At that moment, the band struck up a tune in the drawing room. The party had begun! Marie and Fritz rushed out to greet their guests. Everyone was celebrating merrily, and Marie danced and played with her friends all night long. She showed everyone her Nutcracker, and all agreed he was a most fine specimen.

But Fritz, bragging to his friends, claimed that he would make the Nutcracker crack the biggest nut he could find. And grabbing the Nutcracker from Marie's arms, he forced a giant Brazil nut into the doll's mouth.

Crack! The poor Nutcracker was no match for such a large, hard nut, and his jaw had snapped clean off. Crying out in anger, Marie took the Nutcracker back from a guilty-looking Fritz and brought him to Drosselmeyer, who bound up the doll's jaw with a bit of white silk.

Late that night, when the party was long over, Marie tossed and turned in her bed. She worried about her Nutcracker, all alone where she had left him in the drawing room. Quietly, she crept into the room and scooped him up, settling on the sofa beside the great Christmas tree. Just as she began to drift off to sleep, the grandfather clock struck midnight, and Marie awoke with a start. She heard a terrible rustling and squeaking coming from the walls and turned to see huge mice scurrying across the room toward her!

At once, a figure leapt forward. It was her Nutcracker! But now he was taller than she was, and carrying a sword. At his command, the door from the nursery swung open, and out marched Fritz's toy soldiers to do battle with the mice.

The mice were led by an enormous and evil-looking Mouse King, who advanced on the Nutcracker. The Nutcracker fought bravely, but soon stumbled and fell. Marie jumped to her feet. Without thinking, she pulled off her slipper and threw it as hard as she could at the Mouse King, making him turn in confusion. The Nutcracker saw his chance and dealt a great blow to the giant mouse, toppling him to the ground. The battle was won!

As the frightened mice scurried away, Marie ran to her Nutcracker, to find that he was no longer the wooden doll with the wide smile.

He had been transformed into a fair young man, who smiled at Marie. He explained that he had once been a prince in his own country, but had helped rescue a child from the clutches of an evil sorcerer, the Mouse King. Enraged, the Mouse King had cursed the prince to live as a wooden nutcracker, banished from his own kingdom. Now that the Mouse King had been defeated, the curse was lifted, and the prince invited Marie to join him as he returned to his home in the magical Land of Sweets. Marie took his hand, and a swirling winter wind whisked them both into the night.

When Marie and the Nutcracker Prince arrived in the Land of Sweets, they were greeted by a crowd of hundreds, celebrating the prince's return. A great cheer arose as a carriage of white chocolate carried them to a castle made entirely of gum drops. Once inside, they met

the Sugar Plum Fairy, a beautiful sprite who welcomed them to a special celebration in their honor.

Taking their seats upon thrones made of spun sugar, a parade of dancers and acrobats leapt and whirled before them. Marie could smell the enticing aromas of chocolate, coffee, tea, and ginger as they performed. Finally, the Sugar Plum Fairy called everyone in the hall to join the dance, and Marie and her Nutcracker Prince twirled together alongside the courtiers and dancers. It was the most magical night Marie had ever known. The celebrations ran very late, and Marie couldn't help but return to her seat to rest her head, and as the music played on, her eyes gently closed . . .

Marie awoke in her own bed, with sunlight playing on her face. Was it all just a dream? She ran to the drawing room and discovered—her Nutcracker wasn't there! In fact, she couldn't find him anywhere in the house. Her parents insisted that she must have simply misplaced him. But as Marie sat down with her family to a fine Christmas breakfast, she smiled to herself, for she alone knew the true tale of the Nutcracker Prince.

THE END

Lunch Bag Luminarias

Materials
Brown paper lunch bags
Hole punch
Sand or clean, unscented kitty litter
Tea-light candles (option to use battery-operated tea light candles)
Adult helper

Luminarias are traditional Christmas lanterns popular in Mexico and the southwestern United States. Sometimes they are also called farolitos, meaning "little lanterns." Symbols of welcome and good cheer, they have been lighting pathways and homes since the 16th century! They are great for parties or front porches, but be sure to keep small children and pets a safe distance away.

1. Use a hole punch to punch designs into several paper lunch bags.

2. Pour 2 inches (5 centimetres) of sand or kitty litter into each bag.

3. Put a tea light in the middle of each bag. Firmly press it into the sand.

4. Find a good outdoor spot to line up your luminarias, such as a patio or walkway. Wait for an evening when the wind isn't too strong, then ask an adult helper to light them.

Seek & Find
All Around Town

Find in this scene:

6 reindeer
5 cats
2 giant teddy bears
3 elves

The Nutcracker Prince
The red toy car
The orange balloon
The dog riding the bus

We Wish You a Merry Christmas

We wish you a Merry Christmas,
We wish you a Merry Christmas,
We wish you a Merry Christmas
And a Happy New Year!

Good tidings we bring
To you and your kin.
We wish you a Merry Christmas
And a Happy New Year!

Now bring us some figgy pudding,
Now bring us some figgy pudding,
Now bring us some figgy pudding
And a cup of good cheer!

We won't go until we get some,
We won't go until we get some,
We won't go until we get some,
So bring some right here!

Good tidings we bring
To you and your kin.
We wish you a Merry Christmas
And a Happy New Year!

'TWAS THE NIGHT BEFORE CHRISTMAS,

When all through the house
Not a creature was stirring, not even a mouse;
The stockings were hung by the chimney with care
In hopes that St. Nicholas soon would be there;

The children were nestled all snug in their beds,
While visions of sugar-plums danced in their heads;
And mamma in her kerchief, and I in my cap,
Had just settled our brains for a long winter's nap,

When out on the lawn there arose such a clatter,
I sprang from the bed to see what was the matter.
Away to the window I flew like a flash,
Tore open the shutters and threw up the sash.
The moon on the breast of the new-fallen snow
Gave the luster of mid-day to objects below,
When, what to my wondering eyes should appear,
But a miniature sleigh, and eight tiny reindeer,

With a little old driver, so lively and quick,
I knew in a moment it must be St. Nick.
More rapid than eagles his coursers they came,
And he whistled, and shouted, and called them by name:

"Now, Dasher! now, Dancer! now, Prancer and Vixen!
On, Comet! on, Cupid! on, Donder and Blitzen!
To the top of the porch! to the top of the wall!
Now dash away! dash away! dash away all!"

As dry leaves that before the wild hurricane fly,
When they meet with an obstacle, mount to the sky;
So up to the house-top the coursers they flew,
With the sleigh full of toys, and St. Nicholas too.

And then, in a twinkling, I heard on the roof
The prancing and pawing of each little hoof.
As I drew in my head, and was turning around,
Down the chimney St. Nicholas came
with a bound.

He was dressed all in fur, from his head to his foot,
And his clothes were all tarnished with ashes and soot;
A bundle of toys he had flung on his back,
And he looked like a peddler just opening his pack.

His eyes—how they twinkled! his dimples how merry!
His cheeks were like roses, his nose like a cherry!
His droll little mouth was drawn up like a bow,
And the beard of his chin was as white as the snow;

The stump of a pipe he held tight in his teeth,
And the smoke it encircled his head like a wreath;
He had a broad face and a little round belly,
That shook when he laughed, like a bowlful of jelly.

He was chubby and plump, a right jolly old elf,
And I laughed when I saw him, in spite of myself;
A wink of his eye and a twist of his head,
Soon gave me to know I had nothing to dread;

He spoke not a word, but went straight to his work,
And filled all the stockings; then turned with a jerk,
And laying his finger aside of his nose,
And giving a nod, up the chimney he rose;

He sprang to his sleigh, to his team gave a whistle,
And away they all flew like the down of a thistle.
But I heard him exclaim, ere he drove out of sight,

"Happy Christmas to all, and to all a good night."

57